HARVEST

KRIS WALDHERR

WALKER & COMPANY · NEW YORK

TODAY IS THE DAY I'VE BEEN WAITING FOR.

Today is the harvest.

All year we have worked so hard.

Mom and I planted SEEDS in our garden

and pulled weeds so the SUN could reach it.

We fed it WATER when it was dry.

We put fertilizer into the SOIL when it was hungry.

All year our garden has worked so hard.

It put down strong ROOTS so plants could grow.

It flowered and created FRUIT upon trees.

VEGETABLES and sweet-smelling HERBS grew from our seeds.

Now the fruits and vegetables we harvest today

will feed us later when we are hungry.

I pick APPLES *from the trees*

and dig CARROTS *from the soil.*

I pluck herbs, like SWEET BASIL *and* DILL,

and flowers, like BLACK-EYED SUSANS *and* SUNFLOWERS.

But of all the garden's gifts, the PUMPKINS *are my favorite,*

so smooth and orange upon the vine.

We have a bounty of FOOD *and* FLOWERS.

I feel thankful to the EARTH *for its work, the harvest.*

There's so much—more food than we could eat at one meal!

But there are ways we can store our harvest for later.

Mom and I hang the flowers and herbs to dry.

We bake pies and bread. We cook some of the fruit and store it in glass jars.

That night there is a huge moon, as round and rusty as a pumpkin.

Mom tells me it's called the HARVEST MOON. *I know why.*

We have harvested our garden.

All year we have worked so hard.

All year our garden has worked so hard.

Now it is time to rest.

FOR DAISY MILLER-FUENTES

Special thanks—and an armful of flowers—to Stephanie St. Pierre,
Jessica Clerk, and Rebecca and Lila Cohn for their generous help with this book.

First published in the United States of America in 2001 by
Walker Publishing Company, Inc.
Published simultaneously in Canada by Fitzhenry and Whiteside, Markham, Ontario L3R 4T8

Library of Congress Cataloging-in-Publication Data
Waldherr, Kris.
    Harvest / Kris Waldherr.
        p. cm.
        Summary: A girl and her mother spend the day gathering vegetables, fruit,
and herbs from their garden.
        ISBN 0-8027-8792-4 — ISBN 0-8027-8793-2 (reinforced)
            [1. Gardens—Fiction.] I. Title.
PZ7.W143 Har 2001
[E]—dc21   2001026550

The artist used watercolor and gouache on Arches watercolor paper to create the illustrations for this book.
Book design by Kris Waldherr

Printed in Hong Kong
2 4 6 8 10 9 7 5 3 1